The Weight of Birds

2020 Silver Medal Winner

Contemporary Christian Romance

Reader's Choice Awards

Read the book that started it all!

"…Author Amanda Lewis has crafted a truly uplifting work of romantic and dramatic fiction which keeps emotion and deep personal connection at its core at all times. Realistic and genuine in its presentation of feelings, Cecelia Sweeting is a woman that all can relate to in her pain, and admire for her strength and fortitude moving forward from tragedy." K.C. Finn, for *Reader's Favorite*

Still Waters

Peter's Story

A Sequel to The Weight of Birds

By

Amanda Lewis

Also by Amanda Lewis

The Weight of Birds

<u>Short Stories</u>

The Cimmerian Soldier

George: A Short, Unconventional Story About A Short,
Unconventional Man

To all of my precious readers who requested a sequel,

and to everyone who liked Peter just a little bit more.

Thank you for appreciating my stories!

This one's for you!

And we know that all things work together for good to them that love God, to them who are the called according to His purpose.

Romans 8:28 KJV

Still Waters

Peter's Story

A Sequel to The Weight of Birds

By

Amanda Lewis

Chapter One

about two years later ...

I knew the day I'd lost her. No, the moment. I can pinpoint exactly when the shift happened. In Berlin, in the airport. It was subtle, but I could feel the shift in the atmosphere around me. That little voice in the back of my head said, "You need to seriously consider the consequences of your next words, or you might regret them forever."

She hadn't even known what was about to happen. But I knew. I knew I was about to change her. She was eating apple strudel, lost in her food coma bliss. She was so cute when she got excited about whatever she was eating. Her nose was wrinkled up like a bunny's, and her eyes sparkled before they rolled back in sheer delight. Why had I never told her that? How beautiful she was, how precious she was to me? The most mundane, ordinary things were so much better when she was involved in them.

I had to break the news to her while she was mesmerized by the warm, flaky pastry. I'd been called away for work, to Copenhagen. Not Gothenburg, like we'd planned. She'd be alone with my brother for a week. A week with a stranger in a strange land. If the roles were reversed, I would've probably had a panic attack. I can't live a life unplanned.

A whole week with Mattias could only result in disaster for me. Mattias was the fun one, the charming one. He'd never met a stranger, or an adversary, that he couldn't win over in a matter of minutes. I was the serious one, the professional one, the one who'd always been unable to bend and flow with change.

The last thing I wanted to do was leave her alone with Mattias, leave her alone at all. She'd already lost so much when her life had derailed, experienced pain far beyond what I'd imagined. I'd never leave her on purpose, yet I did, for work of all things. Idiot.

She'd bloomed right before my eyes, the most sacred of treasures and beautiful sights to see. The way she'd found herself, grown to stand on her own two feet. I tried to assist her from a distance, getting a steady stream of professionals into her gallery to get her noticed and retain her independence. I'd given her space to find her footing while assuring her I was there for her. Too much space? Not enough? It hadn't been enough. At the end, I hadn't been enough.

I made it through the wedding, just barely. After Cecelia and Mattias left to do what married couples do, I had eaten twelve hot dogs from Roger's vendor friends to drown my sorrows, complete with all the toppings. I puked out every single one within a few hours. But I was there for her. I was determined to be there for her. It wasn't about me, or Mattias at that point. It was all for her. He was the better man. He won her fair and square. I lost.

He was there for her, complimenting her in ways I never thought possible. I knew it the moment I picked her up at his house, after the week was over. They were melded together, even on opposite sides of the room. I tried to ignore it, pretend I hadn't watched my little brother's reactions for years, but I knew. I saw him trying to stifle the delight in his eyes when he looked at her. He wouldn't have betrayed me on purpose, but he was changed. So was she. It was over for us, but still I kept on.

I lost the love of my life. And then there was Gregory Charles. He should've been mine. I should've talked about God more. I knew faith was important to her, and I knew we had similar beliefs. Why didn't I just tell her? Something that could've bonded us closer? Why had I been so stupid for so long?

Then she was pregnant again, with Ellison Jayne, Ellie for short. A bright and happy girl, with golden curls just like Cecelia's. She's only a year old now but she always looks at me like I'm her favorite person in the whole world.

It still didn't feel real until last month, and then I lost it. She showed up at my apartment, toddler Charlie clinging to her leg, Ellie slung onto her opposite hip. She wanted to tell me the happy news in person; she was three months pregnant with her third baby. Three children, none of which were mine. My brother is the father of the family I wanted, because I wasn't man enough ... Enough ... I wasn't ...

The bottle rolled from Peter's grasp, shattering upon contact with the floor. He was temporarily jarred from his drunken stupor by the sound, long enough to pull the comforter over his head to block out the blinding light of the morning sun.

What seemed like seconds later, but which was actually the next day, he was awakened by the ringing of his cellphone.

"Hellllllooo," he faintly growled, unaware if he'd actually hit the answer button or not.

"Peter? Peter, are you there? It's Mark from Contemporary."

"Whaaaa … aaaaywant?"

"You've got everyone at work talking. Look, I don't know what you've gotten yourself into, but you've got exactly today to wrap it up and get back to work before you're fired. Do you hear me? If you'd just come down here and talk to Petrov instead of ghosting the whole museum, I'm sure she'd be willing to work with you through whatever's going on."

"Whaaat day …"

"What day is it? Peter, good grief. It's Sunday morning. I'm trying to do you a professional courtesy, friend to friend. You'd better be at work tomorrow and you'd better have a great excuse for your behavior this past month. You've missed two weeks and called out sick the other two weeks. If you weren't previously so upstanding and outstanding at your job, you'd have been fired by now. They've written you off as needing personal time but you've got to yank a knot in it. Petrov's patience is wearing thin."

"Yeeeaaahhhhttthankkss."

The phone tumbled to the floor, narrowly missing a puddle of vodka.

Chapter Two

Peter awoke with a jolt at 5 a.m. His head was pounding, but he briefly registered eating some pizza rolls at some point the night before, so it wasn't as bad as it could have been. He stumbled to the mirror and was horrified at what he found staring back at him. His beard was scraggly and chaotic; he hadn't shaved in at least three weeks. He caught a whiff of a foul stench, realizing he hadn't bathed in as long, either. His ice-blue eyes were a dull hum of what they'd been, now sunken and shadowed by depression. His usually slim and trim body had put on about ten pounds on his stomach, purely from vodka and other alcoholic beverages. His hair hadn't grown too much, luckily, so at least that was salvageable. He turned the shower on, steaming up the mirror sufficiently to disguise any other imperfections before he tried to rinse away the last month.

He kept his suits in pristine condition, always. Even during his bout of self-destruction, the suits had remained crisp and unharmed in his closet. Peter selected a light-gray suit, with a black shirt and black belt. The light gray made his translucent skin and dull blue eyes look like those of an undertaker, which matched his mood perfectly. Opting to walk to work to clear his head instead of riding his scooter, Peter set his helmet on the four-foot-tall stack of pizza boxes beside the door before he headed out.

The Met was a good hour's walk from Peter's apartment, almost directly up 8th Avenue and then a short trip across Central Park. He always left early any time he went anywhere, walking or scooting. He may not be a lot of things, but punctual wasn't on that list. When he showed up, that is.

Momentarily frowning at his behavior over this last month, Peter's thoughts were distracted by the glorious smell of rich coffee and baked goods wafting down 8th Avenue. As he got closer to the smell, he deduced it was coming from a new restaurant. He couldn't remember seeing it before, but a lot of people were definitely aware of it. There was a short line out the door, so he quickly stepped in behind the last hungry customer. The sign on the door said, "*Sunny Sides Breakfast and Bakery,*" and it had a repulsive-looking rooster as the mascot. Peter wrinkled his nose. Whoever had designed this logo was clearly not an artist.

The line moved quickly, and inside the room was packed. Two-top tables lined the left-hand side, and all were occupied. Along the right-hand side, three massive menu boards hung over glass cases filled with breakfast items, baked goods, cakes, pastries, cookies, and almost any other tasty snack imaginable.

Peter wanted a cinnamon roll, but opted for sustenance instead. The girl at the counter was a bubbly brunette.

"Welcome to Sunny Sides! What can I get for you?"

"I'll have a coffee, black, and a lox bagel to go."

"All right, that'll be $11.85." She turned to the kitchen assembly line not too far from her and screamed, "SNOOTY PATOOTIE WALKING!"

Peter was horrified. At her screech, at the name she'd given him, at the whole situation.

"I beg your pardon?"

"It's the menu item's name. We use the best Norwegian salmon in our lox bagels, very expensive."

"That's the best you could come up with?"

The clerk ignored his question as she handed him his coffee, wickedly grinning at his unease.

"Condiments are right down there if you'd like to dress up your coffee as you wait."

"Where will I get my order?"

She grinned again, unsettling him. "Don't worry, you won't be hard to find."

*****

Petrov was waiting for him at the elevator. "Eight on the dot, I see. At least you're on time today. My office, now."

Peter followed the woman down the hallway. He felt like a scorned puppy who'd just been whacked on the nose with a rolled-up newspaper. Heads turned with every department he passed. Mark popped out of his office, and Peter gave him a silent '*thank you*' nod.

Myshka Petrov was a demanding woman, the head of the curating department and every bit as intimidating as her name sounded. A good four-and-a-half-feet tall, she towered over no one physically, so she had to make her presence known through her confidence and attitude. At least fifty-five years old, she had had plenty of years to practice strong-arming men twice as tall as her down to gravel at her feet.

Pale white skin, stick-straight white hair, angled features, and eyes as black as onyx, she was as exquisite as she was deadly, like a poisonous viper. Peter figured he was about to be fired for sure. She waited for him to enter her office, closing the door behind him.

"Sit down, Mr. Levander," her tiny frame commanded him. Peter sat instantly.

Petrov sat down across from him, behind her glass-topped desk. It was a modern art piece; the artist escaped Peter's memory at the moment but he recalled a showing within the last year. Each side had a black swirl, functioning as the desk's legs. The rest of the office had been redecorated in various shades of black, white, and red to match it. Petrov's clothing conveniently matched it today as well. A form-fitting black blouse with a ruffle over the button, combined with a tight black-and-white-striped pencil skirt that reached her mid-calf, with red Jimmy Choo's. Everyone whispered that she would've been terribly attractive if she wasn't so scary.

She sized him up and stared him down. Peter looked up to meet her gaze, then dropped his head again. His usual air of confidence had evaporated as soon as he'd seen her at the elevator.

"I understand Mr. Evans was responsible for getting you back to work today." A statement rather than a question.

"He called me yesterday and advised I come talk to you."

"You've missed four weeks of work. Two of those were … uncommunicated." The nice way of saying he just quit showing up. "Explain yourself."

Peter sighed. How was he going to explain this? He'd just lost his mind? Honesty was the best policy?

"I … there were … I had family issues. I got depressed. I really do not have an excuse. I lost my head for a bit, and I am terribly sorry for the inconvenience. I do love my job, but I understand your decision. I will take no more of your time, Mrs. Petrov." He sighed before standing up to leave. *What's done is done.*

"Mr. Levander, sit back down and shut up. Don't use that formal speech cow manure on me; we're behind closed doors. I'm not firing you. I'm trying to help you, but you're making it difficult. I understand difficult times. The museum's policy is that you may take up to two months off for personal leave for mental health, provided you go to therapy. I've taken the liberty of scheduling your appointments for you, with the same therapist many of us here have used." Peter's eyes widened.

"Relax, you only have to go three times for me to be able to count it, it's hardly an inconvenience. Since you voluntarily came in today to demonstrate your devotion to your job, you've allowed me to include the last two weeks as well. Go home, Mr. Levander. Take the next six weeks to get your mind right and be back and ready to go by the week of the Gala."

Peter could hardly believe what he was hearing. Maybe she wasn't as scary as they'd all thought. "Thank you, Mrs. Petrov. Thank you for understanding." He stood up and started to the door.

"Oh, and Mr. Levander, one more thing. For the love of all things good in this world, if you're going to drink vodka, at least buy a decent one. You shame Russia and Sweden with the cheapness I smell oozing out from your pores."

As Peter walked towards the elevator, Mark ran up beside him. "Hey, buddy, everything go ok in there?"

"Everything's fine. Thank you for calling me yesterday, I appreciate it. I'll see you at the Gala."

*****

On the way back to his apartment, Peter decided he'd celebrate by treating himself to the cinnamon roll he'd seen this morning at Sunny Sides. He peered inside at the register before he walked in, unwilling to see the screeching brunette again.

"What can I get for you?" a much more reasonable-sounding person at the register asked him.

"I'll have a coffee, black, and one cinnamon roll, please."

"Would you like extra icing?"

"What? No, regular is fine." *Americans.* Cinnamon buns needed very little, if any, icing if they were made correctly.

"That'll be $4.95."

"Did you charge for the coffee?"

"No, sir. Boss said you look like you've had a bad day so it's on the house."

"Um … ok. Thank you?"

"Thank you and come again!"

*****

Peter went back to his apartment, collecting a massive stack of mail from his downstairs post office box on the way. Now that he'd been out for a minute, he could clearly smell how much he needed to clean up. He opened all the windows, letting the fresher city air filter through his stale apartment. He took out eight bags of garbage, as well as the pizza boxes, down to the dumpster. He then ran two loads each through the dishwasher and laundry. He poured all of the cheap vodka down the sink, at least for today. Then, Peter took an uninhibited nap.

Chapter Three

Peter had a full week before his first therapy appointment, and nothing but time on his hands. He made a quick list of things he'd always wanted to do in the States, and decided that now was as good a time as ever.

By now, Mattias had long since constructed fanciful gallery signs, for both he and Cecelia to hang over their galleries. Cecelia's was *"Sweeting Gallery,"* with detailed, subtle shadows of seagulls in the corners, something you wouldn't notice unless you really knew her. Peter shook his head. That irritating seagull. He tried not to be bitter, but he'd seen it on the balcony plenty of times at her apartment. Didn't that count? It only infuriated him the more he thought about it.

He entered the door directly under the "Levander Gallery" sign. *Real genius name.*

"Hey, brother!" Mattias ran up and hugged him when he entered the gallery. Mattias was always so happy now, so cheerful. It was disgusting, and Peter threw up in his mouth a little bit. "Do you want me to go get Cecelia? Have you heard the news?"

Was he trying to be rude? Undoubtedly, Cecelia had told Mattias that she'd come to visit him. They were disgustingly perfect; he'd bet that they had no secrets from each other at all. They were practically sewn together. Their house was right across the Bay, but they insisted on never being separated. Cecelia now used her old apartment as a makeshift daycare and storage locker. As far as Peter knew, they still had a bed upstairs, too, in case inspiration struck and Mattias got carried away painting late into the night.

"Yes, she told me," Peter said bitterly. "You don't need to get her; I stopped by to see you, actually." Mattias' eyebrows went up, questioningly. "I was just going to let you know that I'm going to be out of town for a few days. I'm going to the Poconos."

"Oh, really?" Mattias' voice got slightly higher. "With someone?"

"No, not with anyone. By myself." *Jerk, rub it in a little deeper.* "I have … some time off so I thought I would spend it seeing the sights. I'm headed out now and just thought you should know."

"Great, well take lots of pictures for Cecelia! You know how she loves selfies."

Peter turned to leave, rolling his eyes in the process.

*****

Once he got out of the city traffic, it was a nice stretch of wide-open land and interstate. Without the congestion constantly around him, Peter started to feel the weight lift off his chest. It'd been a long time since he could see trees in their wild habitat, as God intended. He'd rented a jeep, for all terrain driving in case he got really adventurous. He'd always wanted a manly jeep but it was so impractical to have a car in the city, so he'd resorted to his scooter instead.

Peter had also rented a cabin, in the middle of it all, or rather in the middle of nowhere. Right smack in the middle of the Poconos, and just a stone's throw away from Bushkill Falls, the tiny cabin was locked away from modern society.

The lady on the phone had advised him to bring some groceries with him, because he would be isolated when he got to his cabin. If he was going for a true wilderness retreat, she assured him there was no better place to stay. Peter stopped at a grocery store in East Stroudsburg that looked on the edge of what was left of civilization. He got some lunch meat, bottled water, potatoes, butter, steaks, and a few other various things. The lady had said Peter could rent the cabin for four days minimum, six if he decided he needed more time. He purposely didn't walk down the wine and beer aisle. It was a good week for a cleanse.

By the time Peter got to the cabin, it was late evening. A single floor studio log cabin, if there ever was such a thing, was perfect for a romantic weekend getaway. Or perfect for locking yourself away from the world, whichever purpose suited your needs. The key was under the frog statue in the front flower bed, like the rental lady had said it would be.

Being late March, it was still pretty cold outside, yet the cabin itself looked quiet and homey, beckoning Peter in with solitude's arms open wide. There was a single lamp turned on inside the foyer, to illuminate his arrival.

Peter walked in, and flipped the light switch by the door. An overhead light came on, attached to a giant ceiling fan. He thought about turning it off and then decided against it when he saw a pile of blankets and comforters on the end of the fold-out couch. He put the groceries in the fridge and opened as many windows as he could. There was a sliding glass door leading to the back patio, which overlooked a lake. Peter realized he'd forgotten to do research to find out if there were bears around there, so he decided not to leave any door wide open just in case.

Peter turned off all the lights and pulled the couch out. He pulled off all of his clothes except his boxers, and climbed under four piled-up blankets. He'd done well since leaving the gallery earlier in the day, but as he drifted off to sleep, his last thoughts were of how much Cecelia would've loved it here.

*****

His stomach woke him up from a deep sleep the next day. Peter looked at his phone and saw that it was 10 a.m. He'd been asleep for well over fifteen hours, completely wiped out from exhaustion without the help of any alcohol. He went outside to scout his surroundings. There was a charcoal grill on the patio, and he cursed to himself because he'd forgotten to buy charcoal or matches. Walking back into the kitchen, he was relieved to find a small bag of charcoal, a small bottle of lighter fluid, and a box of matches on the island countertop that he hadn't even seen last night. Attached was a note, "Everyone forgets. Enjoy your week."

One thing Peter had gotten good at over recent years was cooking. In trying to keep up with Mattias in impressing Cecelia, his recipes had been on point. Or so he thought. They may not look fancy by the time they made it to the plate, but they always tasted pretty good.

Peter found a strainer, cutting board, and some aluminum foil underneath the kitchen sink, along with a few other pots, pans, and regular household amenities. He sat the steaks out to get room temperature for a few moments, and smeared a little bit of minced garlic on them. He washed his potato and cut his chives, before wrapping the potato in foil and putting it in the oven. He then went outside to start up the grill.

In an effort to feel closer to Cecelia, he'd started listening to opera. At first, he ridiculously entertained the thought that maybe he could win her back if he could hold a conversation about *Onegin*. Eventually, he realized he really did like opera. *Lakmé* being his favorite, he set up the record player outside and put the record on he'd brought with him. "The Bell Song" echoed over the landscape.

After he'd eaten lunch and was sufficiently full, Peter walked down to the lake. At this point, he was and had stayed only in his boxers. With no one around, who was there to care about formality in the wilderness? Even though it was cold, Peter was Scandinavian, so the weather felt like summer to him. He felt the earth and the leaves crunch under his bare feet as he walked towards the lake. It had rained at some point in the night, he guessed. The ground was slick beneath him, and the twigs and leaves had the unmistakable sheen of fresh rain.

There was an old story—or maybe not so old, he couldn't remember—he'd heard at the museum about how bare feet absorb the nutrients and minerals in the ground and distribute them throughout your body. That was why any indigenous peoples or cultures, including Native Americans, had better immune systems and lower rates of mental health issues. Peter stood there, barefoot beside the lake, imagining he was absorbing all the goodness the earth had to give him. He didn't need a lot; he always tried not to be a burden on anyone, instead choosing to take care of everyone around him. But maybe this once he could take just a little bit of extra help for himself.

Treading slowly on the rocks that directly bordered his patch of lake, Peter maneuvered until he found a flat spot, enough for a makeshift beach. He inched into the water, first letting it wash over his toes. The first wave, if he could call it that, took his breath away and he started laughing. It was so cold and piercing, and it made him think of his childhood when he, Mattias, and their youngest brother Caspar had done the polar plunges in Gothenburg in the dead of winter. Peter threw back his head and laughed a deep, aching belly laugh for the first time since he could remember. He walked into the lake, commanding the water to embrace him.

He came up screaming after he'd dunked himself head first into the dark liquid ice. Peter looked around the edge of the lake, but there was no one there to hear his screams. The only life he could see were two deer at the far edge of the lake, puzzled by all the ruckus.

Acclimating to the temperature after a moment, Peter swam over to a floating log. The few turtles who'd been sunbathing on top and minding their own business hopped off dramatically as he approached them. He draped his shoulders around the slimy, soggy, moss-covered bark, and kicked his way out further into the lake. The lake was calm and serene, like a black sapphire underneath him. Looking into it, Peter could only see his reflection, and the faint outline of his legs as he treaded. His face was starting to look a little better, and his eyes were a little less sunken in.

Occasionally, Peter would feel some sort of fish brush by his leg, or a turtle head butt him in vengeance. Otherwise, he was alone with his thoughts. He decided he wasn't going to spend these few solitary days dwelling on Cecelia, because he'd wasted enough time doing that already. What was and what never could've been didn't matter anymore, there was nothing he could do to change it. Would he change it if he could? She was so radiant around Mattias, and she'd grown so confident.

Likewise, Mattias was a completely different person now to the brother he'd grown up with. Though still plenty creative and always the life of the party, now Mattias was dependable, responsible. He'd invested in stocks, bought them a house right across the river, and made sure they had all the types of insurance a person could ever need. He'd finally done all of the things adults were supposed to do. Really, if he was honest about it, Peter was immensely proud of Mattias. Plus, there was no denying that Mattias was a natural-born father. He radiated love, patience, and understanding to the point that it was pathetic.

Peter floated in the lake until the sun crossed over and the trees' shadows had turned around. He returned the log to its rightful owners and made his way back to the shoreline. Peter looked down and pinched his small but noticeable belly roll that had appeared over the past several weeks. He was going to have to do more than float around if he wanted to get back into his slim and trim shape. That was a problem for later.

He dragged himself back up through the woods to the cabin, not wanting to leave nature behind. Feeling emotionally drained, but mentally rejuvenated after his soak in the lake Peter changed into dry pajamas and climbed back under his four heavy blankets.

The next morning, Peter woke up at the crack of dawn, refreshed and full of energy. He made himself do 300 sit-ups before he did anything else. Then he pulled out the travelers' maps, and determined that the lake turned into a creek that he could follow for as far as he dared and do some magnificent hiking. He packed some bread, cheese, and bottled waters, and headed out.

The ground was drier than it had been the previous day, which helped the grip of the terrain out immensely. Peter walked along the creek for as much as he could, occasionally stopping to look at this mushroom or that wildflower. By the sun, Peter guesstimated he'd hiked about six hours, maybe slightly less, when he heard heavy footsteps. He'd come to a part of the creek where the water flow was steadier and more hushed. Across on the other side, he could hear someone moving around. They weren't talking, but their steps sounded purposeful and sure. Peter stopped and peered, expecting some other hiker to come out from behind the tree and wave. Who, or what, showed up, was an entirely different experience.

First there were the ears, black and fuzzy, that popped out sideways from behind one side of the tree, like the grammatical colon. Then a fuzzy black ball rolled down that same tree, splatting onto the ground with its legs splayed out in starfish formation. The first cub came from behind and tackled the fallen cub, and they rolled around on the ground, growling at each other for a split second. Peter was in awe of them, and quickly pulled out his phone and took a few pictures. He was shooting a short video when he realized he was still hearing the heavier footsteps, which didn't match the babies' sounds as they were wrestling on the ground.

Mom showed up a few seconds later, about the same time that Peter realized he was in an open area and not a zoo. His mouth fell open as she looked at him, their eyes making contact across the creek. She took a step forward; Peter took a step back. His mind frantically raced, trying to remember anything at all that he might've seen on TV about how to handle a bear encounter so that he wouldn't end up as a nice Peter-skinned rug in her den. His mind hit a dead end at every turn as she took another step towards him. All he could think was to move slowly, and to try not to look too much like a salmon. He moved at a snail's pace to put his phone in his backpack, and then he raised his hands up in submission, as if to say, *"I'm sorry I'm in your territory, I'm leaving now."* The bear raised her head at him, an air of regality in her gesture. *"I'll allow it,"* Peter imagined her saying, as he continued to back away. The babies tumbled into the edge of the water, making waves around themselves, right as Peter turned his back to the family. He was done hiking for the day.

Chapter Four

When he got back, Peter took another dip in the lake to rinse away the remainder of his fear. Two more days here would probably be plenty. He didn't want to risk running into anything else that could use his ribs as toothpicks.

Momentarily, Peter had gotten lost in a rabbit hole of thoughts as he spiraled downwards. *Who would have heard me scream? Would anyone have ever found my body? How would Cecelia have felt if I had died?* He slept in late, tired from his near-death experience. When he woke up the next day, he made a mental note to quit using alarm clocks on his off days. Somehow, he'd never realized how stressed out the simple task of watching a clock had made him. Why? What for? So he could be at the next place on time? Just to leave that place to then be at the next, next place? It was an endless cycle that he didn't enjoy, and it did not enrich his life at all.

Firing up the grill to cook the remaining steaks, Peter did another 300 push-ups to kill time while he waited. He hadn't weighed himself, but he'd always had a fairly fast metabolism and he felt slightly lighter. If not physically, at least mentally. Clean air and no alcohol were working wonders on his psyche.

When he walked back out, a seagull was sitting on the handcrafted wooden table at the end of the patio. He could see it had no right foot, and he didn't need to walk further to know what the rest of it looked like.

"Go away."

The bird sat and stared at him. Peter walked closer.

"What is it she calls you? Birdbrain? You're not wanted here, Major Birdbrain. I said go away!"

The seagull squawked at him in defiance and didn't move. Peter screamed at the bird, who just looked at him with a blank expression. Peter screamed a second time, even louder.

"AHHHHHHHHHHHHHHHHH!" he shouted, waving his arms around, trying to scare the bird away.

"SQUUAAWWK!" The gull fluttered its wings but didn't leave.

"Fine. Stay. I'll leave. I couldn't care less about what you do. I'm not feeding you, either. I've had enough of wildlife this week." And with that, Peter finished cooking his steaks and took them inside.

That afternoon, Peter rummaged through his carefully packed clothes until he found his sketchbook. He'd packed it just in case. He always brought it with him, as a comfort more than anything. It stayed in lining the bottom of his suitcase, never moving. Today, it moved. He'd drawn ever since he was little, and never told many people about it. Drawing was like his diary, something he kept private, for his eyes only. He opened the sliding glass doors and stepped out onto the patio. The intention was to sketch the lake, but the seagull was still on the table. Of course it was.

Peter walked over to the table and sat down on the opposite end from the gull. He was about four feet away from it, maybe less. Peter sighed and flipped to a blank page in his sketchbook.

"Hold still."

The bird stood there, watching him intently with its birdy little eyes. Peter started to sketch him, with the lake in the background.

"You know, you've got a lot of nerve showing up here. You're basically the reason I'm here anyway. Yeah, I know your story. You fly around saving everyone but me. I bet she even sent you here, didn't she? Do you have a message taped to your leg like a messenger pigeon? Are you a messenger gull? Don't for one second consider that I think you're God, or Charlie, or whatever your story is today. I think you're full of it. Just some stupid bird that found a sweet and willing girl to feed you biscuits. Yeah, that's right. That's what I think. Then you got all your gull friends to find doppelgangers in your stupid gull network, so you could rig up this elaborate storyline that even your tiny, pea-sized bird brain would be smart enough to figure out."

The bird just looked at him.

"Oooh yeah, did I hurt your little bird feelings? I thought you were a major. You're supposed to be tough. Why did you leave me behind? You stupid bird; if you have all these great healing powers, why did you break me? I needed a whole ten weeks off work. Ten weeks! Can you even imagine? What's your lifespan, Bird? Is that longer than you've lived? Don't answer that. I don't know, either, and I'm not going to bother to research you. You're just a bird."

The bird blinked slowly, trying not to fall asleep.

"Am I boring you? Were you not sent here to comfort me? Are you not a therapy bird? I have to go to therapy now! That's something I never thought I'd say in my lifetime. Therapy, to talk about my feelings, because I missed work. Why did I miss work? Did you even think to ask? No, you didn't, but I'll tell you. Cecelia is pregnant again – for the third time – and I don't know, I guess something in me just snapped. You knew that already if you've been watching her, and I guess you know that thanks to you, she and Mattias got married. Way to go, Bird. My whole entire life, I've only ever tried to do the right thing, tried to take care of everyone around me and put their needs first. What did I get? What did you give me? A broken heart and nearly fired, that's what you gave me. The short end of the stick, that's what you gave me."

The seagull let out a tiny squawk.

"Oh, you're sorry? That's all you've got to say for yourself? Is that what you came here to say? Or did you come here to rub it in my face and gloat? I almost got eaten by a family of bears yesterday, what would've you done then? Squawk around until someone heard you and found my chewed-up body? No. You would've done nothing, that's what. This was supposed to be my alone time, to heal. Alone. Just me and nature, not me and Cecelia's little gull scout. Are you going to report back to her that I'm completely broken and lost? That I'm out here trying to find myself? I bet you are. You know what? You can go now. Just go on. I'm sure you'll both have a great chat about me on the balcony."

The bird looked at him square in the eyes, fluffed its wings, and flew away. Peter hid his head in his hands for a few minutes. Angry at how he was feeling, and worried because he'd just had an entire conversation with a seagull. He stood up, stripping down to his boxers in the process, and headed down to the lake.

Peter swam laps back and forth in the lake for the rest of the day, until the only light he could see was the one he'd left on in the cabin.

The next day, he packed up what little stuff he had, tidied the cabin as best as he could, and headed back down the mountain. After the seagull had showed up, Peter was left feeling angry and helpless. Instead of feeling relaxed and refreshed, Peter just felt suffocated. He decided he wasn't going to mention the seagull to Cecelia, for fear of a lecture. He just couldn't take a lecture from her.

In the travelers' brochures, he'd seen a place where kids could get kits to mine for gemstones. He decided to stop in and get two to take home to Charlie and Ellie.

Chapter Five

"How was your week?" Dr. Dockett asked. She was a tiny woman, not more than four feet tall. She was tinier than even Petrov, which Peter didn't think was humanly possible. She was at least seventy, with obviously dyed black hair cut straight across, chin length in a bob. She had huge wire-rimmed glasses, like two coasters stacked side by side, and neon pink flip-flops.

"It started out fine."

"And then?"

"And then it wasn't."

"How so?"

"It was relaxing, and then it wasn't."

She leaned forward in her chair. "Listen, Peter. To be frank, in order for these therapy sessions to count, you're going to have to open up. If I mark in your files that you were uncooperative, you're just going to have to come to more, so you might as well nip it in the bud now."

"I thought therapy was confidential."

"Everything you say is confidential, yes. Everything you tell me stays between us. I still have to report to your work that you did or did not make it to your appointments, and that you have or have not made improvements to your mental health. Help me help you."

Peter sighed. "I slept a lot, and I swam a lot. I went hiking one day and encountered a bear family. That was terrifying. I tried not to draw attention to myself and I managed to get away before the mom got really angry." He thought carefully about his next sentences and how to phrase them so that she wouldn't think he needed even more therapy. "And I sketched a bird on the last day before I came home. I would've stayed an extra day, but I'd had enough nature by that time."

"By the time you sketched a bird?"

"Yes."

"Sketching the bird was enough to make you want to come home?" *Why was she focused on the bird?*

"Yes."

"What kind of bird was it?"

"It was a seagull. With no right foot."

"No right foot? How would you suppose he lost his right foot?"

"I don't know. She thinks it was in the Great Gull War." He'd heard the story several times.

"Who is the 'she' you're referring to?" *Quit oversharing, Peter.*

Peter ran his hands through his golden locks. "All right, look, you don't want to hear the long version, so I'll shorten it for you. I fell in love, but I didn't tell her how I felt, not soon enough. Maybe it would've mattered, maybe not. She ended up marrying my brother, and now they're pregnant with their third kid. My brain just lost it, you know? I just lost it. Anyway, there's this seagull. She thinks it's God flying around watching out for us."

"I see. And what do you think about this seagull?"

"I don't know. I mean, most of the time I think it's just a seagull and maybe she's just reading too much into it. But my brother started to believe her, believe her stories. The stupid seagull started following him and now they're married. So, I feel like I didn't see the obvious signs in front of me. Which really makes me mad if I'm being completely honest, because I've spent my life trying to plan on certainties and I lost it all due to a bird, because the bird didn't take my side? That's a little bit preposterous. And of course you can't argue with a bird, because it's a bird."

The therapist sat silent for a few minutes, thinking of what best to say.

"So, you came home early because you got into an argument with a bird?"

"When you put it like that, it does sound crazy. I'm not crazy."

"I don't think you're crazy, Peter. I think you're tightly wound. And I think you're having a midlife crisis. You've felt the need to try and control your surroundings your whole life, and now you're realizing maybe that didn't have the intended effect that you wanted. So, you're lashing out. It's completely normal, almost healthy under the circumstances. Most people buy a sports car or date someone barely out of diapers, but you've decided on the path of self-destruction, which is not all right.

"You have some time off from work. Here's what I want you to do. Between now and our next session, I don't want you to plan anything for yourself except being on time for your next appointment. I want you to wake up every day and do whatever you feel like doing. Additionally, everything that comes your way, say 'yes' to. Especially if your first inclination is to say 'no.' It will take practice, being mentally aware of your responses. Do you understand?"

"Yes."

"You're a fast learner. See you next Wednesday at 3 p.m. sharp."

*****

Peter had, since last week, already decided that he was going to walk everywhere. He enjoyed seeing people on the street, and taking his time getting from place to place. Plus, the exercise alone was relaxing. With less alcohol consumption and his renewed exercise regimen, his middle had noticeably receded already.

Peter walked by Sunny Sides, and noticed there was no line. He decided he wanted coffee and a cinnamon roll, so that's what he got. After fixing his coffee at the condiment table, he sat down at a table to wait on his order.

"Hey there! You're back!" The clerk from the first visit popped over to his table. She pulled out the chair opposite him and sat down, uninvited. Peter groaned internally and started to say something, before remembering he was supposed to be going with the flow. He smiled politely instead.

"Fan of the cinnamon rolls?" She was cute enough; he could see with the light shining through it that her hair was a deep auburn red rather than brown like he'd previously thought. Unless she'd dyed it since. Who cared? He certainly didn't. She was younger than him, but not as young as Cecelia. She had curves in all the right places and she was about as tall as Cecelia. He shook the thoughts out of his head. He was there for the cinnamon roll, and the cinnamon roll alone. Besides, this woman seemed too reckless for him.

"Yes, thank you."

She stared at him for a moment, her eyes slightly squinting at him and the hint of a grin flickering across her full lips. Peter felt himself squirming in her gaze, like an earthworm about to be devoured by a hungry bird. Her lips parted slightly, as if she wanted to say something, before she decided against it. She stood up and held out her hand instead, saying, "Let me know if I can get you anything else. My name's Emma."

"Peter." He reached out to shake her hand. She had a strong, firm grip, not what he'd expected from a coffee clerk. She grabbed his coffee cup and refilled it for him before he'd even noticed. "One sugar or two?"

"Two, please. Thank you."

"Not a problem, honey, here's your order." She reached around the counter and grabbed the bag before placing it and the replenished coffee in front of him.

"Come back and see me, ok?"

"I will."

Did that count as saying yes to a plan? Crap. Maybe I shouldn't leave my apartment. I'm definitely turning my phone on silent so Cecelia and Mattias can't call.

*****

The next morning, Peter went back to Sunny Sides. This time he took his sketchpad, to draw whatever he saw that inspired him. Since living in New York, he'd envied the artists who could just travel around the city, drawing whatever they pleased and making a living off of it. Today, he was going to be one of them. He didn't see Emma, not that he was looking for her. He ordered his usual coffee and cinnamon roll, and selected a table by the window. This time, Peter had brought colored pencils as well. He'd had to dig them out from the depths of his closet, but eventually he'd found them. He began sketching the inside of Sunny Sides, from the door to the coffee station.

When he was done, he got up, walked to Central Park, and sketched a whole new scene. Every day for the next several weeks, all Peter did was walk around the city sketching various scenes and people. If he wanted to eat, he ate. If he wanted dessert, he got it. If he wanted to take a nap on a park bench, that's what he did. Peter just lived.

Chapter Six

"How do you think these last three weeks have gone?" Dr. Dockett asked. She was wearing a neon pink cardigan, making her look more like a lollipop than a professional.

"I think they've gone well. I feel relaxed, uninhibited."

"Great! That's really great, and I'm really proud of the progress you've made. Moving forward, I want you to keep saying 'yes!' Just keep your options open and don't shut everything down instantly, ok? Your final step is to go out on a date."

"I—no, I don't think that's necessary. There's not even anyone I'm interested in." *At all. How is that even part of therapy?*

"I'm not saying get on a dating app or whatever you kids are doing these days. I'm saying if you meet a nice woman, and the two of you strike up a nice conversation, ask her out for coffee. That's all." She shrugged her shoulders and lifted her hands above her like it was just that easy to meet someone. "If you meet a nice woman, ask her out. If a nice woman asks you out, say yes to her. You don't have to marry her and father

her children, Peter. It doesn't have to be all or nothing. Sometimes it can just be coffee. Or a slice of pie. Or whatever, I don't care, just do it." *Note to self, avoid all women.*

"Sure, no problem."

*****

The theme for the Met Gala was Impressionism. Having been welcomed back to his job with a clean slate from Dr. Dockett, Peter had been hard at work making sure the night was a success. It wasn't his department, it was Costume's big night, but the other curators were usually on staff support, supervising some aspect so that Costume could focus on the main event. Peter preferred to stay behind the scenes. Glitz wasn't really his thing, but it was mandatory that they all dress up.

He had a Burberry tux he'd bought the first year he'd been hired, and he'd used it every year since then. He was completely aware that recycled tuxes were a fashion faux pas, but he didn't care. It was classy and timeless, it held up well, and he always stayed out of sight anyway should anyone notice him being out of season.

This year, he'd been demoted to valet supervisor due to his troubles, but he didn't mind. This allowed him to stay outside and away from the crowd, and he really didn't have to talk to anyone except the valets. After all the guests had arrived and the event had started, Peter worked his way into the back hallway, helping the waitstaff keep trays refilled.

The European and Islamic department curators were responsible for coordinating the food this year, and Peter was beyond thankful. The absolute worst thing was the year he'd had to coordinate the dinner. He'd failed to ensure that the shrimp had been deveined, that the canapés had been properly toasted, and that the parsley was to size specifications. It was a disaster of epic proportions. That was the first and last time he'd been assigned to oversee the dinner. He'd gladly take valet any day of the week.

The dinner theme was French hors d'oeuvres and pastries, to match the Impressionism theme. When Peter walked in, the waitstaff were all abuzz with filling their trays to maximum capacity. They were on the savory portion of the evening, and tiny ramekins filled with garlic buttered escargot were being syphoned out of the kitchen in an assembly line fashion to be delivered and re-collected as fast as possible. The plates that held the starters – fromage blanc spread and an onion and goat cheese tart – were already being collected as fast as the hot ramekins were being distributed.

Next on the menu was a tuna, tomato, and basil tartare. Peter peered into the kitchen and saw a line of five expo chefs rapidly packing tablespoons of a pink substance, so as to form the delicate mounds of tiny portions onto tiny plates with a faultless basil leaf on top for a garnish. He hadn't seen the pastries yet, but from experience he knew the dessert crew was in the back, hard at work making their masterpieces picture perfect.

The night continued on, as the hors d'oeuvres and desserts made their circle of life from the kitchen to the dining room to the dish room. Eventually, there were only a few guests left, partying early into the morning. It was about 3 a.m., and most of the event and kitchen staff had long since cleaned up and left by the time Peter started checking the museum and making sure everything was as it should be. Peter made his way to the back of the museum. When he got to the back, there was a van with a familiarly ugly rooster logo backed up into the service door. *What on earth?*

"Hello, Peter." A familiar voice greeted him before he saw the face to match. She was dressed in a white chef's jacket lined with large black buttons; puffy, pinstriped black and white pants; and black, clog-looking shoes. Her wavy auburn hair was stuffed up into a puffy chef's hat.

"Emma? What're you doing here?" Peter realized it came out sounding derogatory, though he didn't mean it that way.

"Oh, well, I see we've reverted to Snooty Patootie mode. It's nice to see you again, thanks for bothering to remember my name, at least. Did you happen to see the dessert centerpiece?" She huffed as she stuffed the box she was carrying into the back of the van and shut the door.

Irritated, Peter deflected. "First of all, your boss probably wouldn't appreciate you talking to your customers like that. Second of all, no, I did not see any centerpieces. I was working the event and I didn't see much of the desserts outside of the puff pastries."

"Well, first of all, no; she welcomes my witty retorts and banter when someone steps out of line to disrespect me. Second of all, how could you have missed it? It was literally a centerpiece!" Clearly offended, she pulled her phone out and furiously scrolled to a picture to show him. "This! You missed *this?*"

Peter's jaw fell open. Indeed he had not missed it. It was a massive urn, full of beautiful flowers. He'd thought it was just another urn, nothing particularly special. It didn't make sense for her to be there, though. What was she doing making centerpieces instead of breakfast? "I wasn't disrespecting you. How did I disrespect you? And I'm not understanding. Why are you here making centerpieces and floral arrangements in your van? Shouldn't you be at your restaurant, you know, making bagels?"

"Making bagels! Ha!" She slammed the door loudly and marched over to the driver's side door. She started to step up into the van. Peter was utterly confused by this point.

"Wait, Emma! I'm sorry. Clearly I've said something to make you mad and I have no clue what that something was."

She stepped back down out of the van, her voice quieting as low as her now sagging shoulders. "No, I'm sorry. I've been up for over twenty-four hours trying to get this perfect and I'm a little testy."

The therapist's voice popped into his head at that moment. "Would you like to go get a cup of coffee and talk about it?" As tired as he was, he was off the next day, so it didn't really matter. Emma stood there staring at him, and Peter couldn't decide if she was deciding on what to say or sleeping with her eyes open. "Tell you what, how about you sit down here on the grass and I'll go get the coffee. It's not too far away, it won't take long. You can close your eyes and rest for a minute."

"I turn—" Emma waved in the general direction of the van. She was going down fast and he definitely couldn't let her drive in that condition.

"I'll turn it off, don't worry," Peter assured her, as he left her side for just a minute to turn the van off and close the access door. If she'd left anything in the kitchen, he'd get it for her later. He put his arm around her shoulders and steered her to a dark, grassy spot underneath a tree, shielded away from the city's bright lights. He propped her up against the tree and draped his Burberry tux jacket over her. "I'll be right back."

Peter kept her van keys with him in case she got any ideas about trying to leave when she could barely form a sentence. *Does this count as a date?* He was going to count it, because a woman asleep against a tree was about all he could handle emotionally. He walked the block or so to the coffee shop, the only one that he knew of that was open and accommodating to the early birds and night owls.

When Peter returned to the tree, Emma was fast asleep. She was wearing his jacket backwards as a makeshift blanket, with her arms wrapped through the sleeves and around her body. She looked too peaceful to move, but Peter didn't want to leave her there alone by herself in the twilight hours of the city, either. He slowly sat down next to her, careful not to disturb her or spill the beverage tray containing the coffees and various additives all over himself. Her head was thrown back at an awkward angle against the tree, so Peter gently moved her so that her temple was resting against his shoulder instead.

The next time Peter opened his eyes, there was hazy light all around the park. Peter rubbed his eyes, trying to remember how he'd ended up outside under a tree in the first place. His watch said it was 6:30 a.m. The beverage tray was beside him, still upright but its contents long cold. He looked down at the warmness that encased his right side. Emma was nuzzled against him, her body hugging his. Her head had moved to the softer part between his shoulder and his chest, and one arm was draped over his stomach. She was snoring lightly, but a serene smile gave away her pleasant dreams.

This was the first time Peter had seen her, really seen her, up close. The chef's hat had long since fallen off, revealing a mass of auburn waves piled haphazardly on her head. A colorful scarf had previously been wrapped around like a headband to keep her hair in check, but it too had wriggled free of its duties and was now carelessly tangled in her hair. She had a round face, full lips, and a cute button nose covered in barely noticeable freckles. Soft, delicate lines around her eyes and mouth betrayed that she was at least in her mid-thirties. Asleep, she looked beautifully fragile, as if she needed protecting. Peter pushed the thought out of his head. He was tired of attracting fragile women who needed to be protected. Not just tired, but exhausted. He was lost in the thought when Emma stirred awake.

"What … happened? Where are we?" she asked, looking around.

"You were worn out after the Gala. I went to get you coffee," he said, holding up the cold cups of liquid, "and by the time I got back you were fast asleep."

"So, you stayed here with me all night?" Emma asked, sitting upright, realizing she was still hugging Peter's body in an intimate embrace.

"I did. You were too tired to drive, and too peaceful to move. I couldn't just leave you here alone in the park. Do you need to call work? I'm sure your boss is furious." He fished in his pocket for his cellphone.

"I'm my own boss, and I'm off today anyway. Don't you have somewhere to be?"

"I don't, actually. I'm off today, too." He handed her the cup of coffee. "Sorry, it's a little cold now."

"I think cold coffee is better anyway. I like a little coffee with my cream." Emma smiled with delight as she rummaged out all of the creamer and most of the sugar from the tray. "Oh, I'm sorry, did you already get yours?"

"Help yourself." Peter smiled at her. It was nice to be around a woman who actively took what she wanted.

"Aaahhhhh …" Emma let out a long sigh as she chugged the liquid down. She rubbed her temples.

"You really should call your boss," Peter urged her again.

"I already told you, I *am* my own boss. I own Sunny Sides."

"Oh! I thought you meant figuratively, not literally. Why were you at the Gala then?"

Emma defensively snapped at him as she'd done the night before, "Why? Sunny Sides not hoity-toity enough for Snooty Patootie's workplace? Should I whip you up some hollandaise to go with your lox before you take me seriously?"

That would probably be delicious. "I really wish you would quit calling me that. That's not what I meant, and I'm about tired of you snapping at me for no reason. Why was a restaurant owner who cooks breakfast foods and pastries at one of New York's glitziest events? It doesn't seem like your cup of tea." Peter realized as he said the words that he'd answered part of his own question. She must've been the one supplying all of the handmade French pastries for the event, but he couldn't back down now.

She read the thought on his face and called him on it, "Looks like you just figured it out, Sherlock." She pulled her phone out of her chef's pants and scrolled through the pictures. Peter remembered that she'd been ranting about an urn the night before. "I was working on this all week; it was the main dessert centerpiece last night. Fondant, buttercream, pastillage, gum paste, the works. My crew and I made the flowers. We hand-painted and detailed them all, petal by petal, leaf by leaf, baby's breath by baby's breath. Painstakingly long days and even longer nights, and then three days ago I started to work on the urn. That was more fondant and marzipan surrounding sponge cake. Shaped, carved, molded, formed, textured, painted, and detailed. I had two assistants working on it, and I estimated over the past two weeks it took no less than at least 500 hours."

Peter's mouth fell open in shock. He never knew that was possible. "That's not cake, Emma. That's *art*. That's pure art!"

She beamed for a second, soaking in his compliment. "Thank you, Peter. Yes, this is art. Cake is art in general."

"Cake is not art. Cake is cake, but *this*? *This* is art." He didn't mean to offend her again, but he knew he had when her brows wrinkled in frustration at him.

"Wrong ... Cake out of a box and into a pan with boxed icing slapped on it is not art. That's just cake. Anything created is art. In general, any custom cake *IS* art, as a matter of fact. Think about it. What is art? Someone's idea, made real. Bridges, buildings, floor designs, floor plans, blueprints, paintings, quilts, furniture, clothes, books, movies, jewelry, even cupcakes. Anything that started as an idea first and then was created into the world is in fact art. It doesn't matter what form it's in. Plus, my great grandfather was Solomon Guggenheim, so that's how I got the job."

Peter looked at her, stunned. Her great grandfather founded the Guggenheim Museum? "Really?"

Emma threw back her head and cackled like a mad hen, "No, but I bet you just messed your pants a little, didn't you?! You should've seen the look on your face!"

"Ok, I think we're done here," Peter said, as he started to get up. "Have a nice day, Emma."

She put her hand on his arm, gesturing for him to stay. "Oh, lighten up. I was only trying to get a rise out of you, silly. You're so uptight and serious, live a little."

There was that word again. *Uptight.* "And you're a little crass."

"Just a little, but I wasn't always. I just got tired of sugar-coated lies."

"So, you started making sugar-coated confections instead."

"Hey, there he is! You made a joke! I knew you had some humor in you somewhere," Emma teased Peter, lightly punching him on the arm.

Peter smiled. "So, how does a fiery woman like you end up owning your own restaurant, anyway?" He was trying to say 'yes' and be open to what life offered him, as per his therapist's suggestion. Right now, life was offering a chatty entrepreneur with a knack for crafting sweets.

"I'll take feisty as a compliment, thank you very much! It actually started with my ex-husband. The name is a slap in his face."

"Oh?"

"Yep. D-I-V-O-R-C-E-D," she said, in an easy Southern drawl Peter hadn't noticed before. "We were high school sweethearts. I don't recommend it. I can't look back on any of those years without seeing his ugly face all over my memories. Anyways, he was the quarterback, so you know he was a real jerk wad from the start. Thought he was all that, and his parents thought so, too. His daddy was a big uppity doctor in town, on several boards of blah blah blah …" She waved her hands around animatedly for emphasis.

"We got married straight out of high school, because I was pregnant. Shotgun wedding and the whole deal. We loved each other then, but we weren't compatible. At all. And our families weren't compatible, either. He gets a football scholarship, and I just apply at the local community college to take basic classes because I assume I'm gonna have to work at the gas station and take care of this baby while he goes and betters himself, right? That's what happens to the women in our town, more often than not.

"Now, I'm the youngest of three girls, so technically I had built-in babysitters already, but I didn't want to utilize that tool unless necessary, you know? I was gonna take care of my child, be the best mother I could be."

Peter nodded his head, trying to take mental notes of everything. "Then what happened?"

"Then what happened was he got hurt in the first game of the season. Some guy as big as an eighteen-wheeler sacked him and snapped his knee right in half. Goodbye scholarship, goodbye football, goodbye decently happy marriage. I was six months pregnant at the time, and now I had this crippled, angry man living in my house, screaming at me constantly. He blamed it on me, got really mad and said it was all my fault because if it hadn't been for me, he would've applied to Michigan or somewhere big, followed Tom Brady's footsteps or some such bull like that. Then one night, we were screaming and arguing and he hit me. I'd already been so stressed out as it was, and then when he hit me I lost my footing and fell down the stairs. I only fell down two stairs, it wasn't like he was purposely trying to kill me, but it was enough …" Emma took a deep sigh.

"I miscarried that night. There were several complications from it, and long story short, the doctor said I couldn't have kids ever again. Hubby felt really bad, said he was going to change. And he did, for a while. He got a mechanic's degree and got a job at the local car dealership doing oil and filters and whatnots. I wanted to adopt, but he didn't, so I drowned myself in baking. I got a job as the lunch lady at our old school, and I made cupcakes for the kids at church every week. People placed orders from me, asked me to participate in bake sales. Food was what I really enjoyed, you know? My ex and I had grown even more distant, so I filled the void with food. I gained some weight in the process," she said, as she pinched her stomach roll, which was about as round as a tube of lip-gloss between her fingers. She had curves in all the right places, and curved inward around her waist. Peter had tried not to notice her perfect hourglass figure since he'd met her, but sitting this close to her for so long, it was becoming impossible.

"I was a lot bigger back then," she said, acknowledging her exaggeration. "Running around starting businesses really melts the weight right off. So anyway, I didn't tell his parents I couldn't have kids. It wasn't any of their business, and of course they never even bothered to ask me. I was just supposed to be an incubator for their heirs. But every time we saw them, every time there was a family get-together or whatever, inevitably it would come up. 'So-in-so is having a baby, isn't that wonderful?' 'So-in-so now has five grandchildren!' Sometimes it would be direct. 'So-in-so is having a baby shower, when do you think you'll be having one?' Of course, my husband wouldn't defend me or say anything to the contrary. He'd just leave me to rot in the corner in my own misery."

"Emma, I'm so sorry," was all Peter could think to say.

"It is what it is. Like I said, I was a lot fatter. He'd mention it frequently, take little jabs at my appearance or how I walked or held myself, just whatever he could notice that would deflate me a little more down to his level. Then, that flea on a rat started cheating on me. Can you believe it? *He* started cheating on *me*, after all he'd put me through. With some fake-tanned, bottle-blonde, pockmarked, meth-addicted tramp no less! She looked more like a block of sharp cheddar with mold growing on it than she did a woman.

"By then, my parents were well clued into my misery and offered to let me move back home, but I wasn't going to take two steps back. I told him I was going to go to culinary school and open my own restaurant, like I'd always dreamed of. I knew I'd be good at it. Of course, he told me I couldn't, that I'd never amount to anything of note and I'd never be able to do anything without him. I applied and started taking classes. I'd saved up my lunch lady money so I could pay for myself, another fact that he hated because I was proving that I could be independent without him.

"Finally, on the last day, he was taunting me and telling me how I wouldn't be anything if it weren't for him. I said, 'Well, I got news for you, honey, this ain't my circus anymore and I'm tired of cleaning up your elephant dung.' Then he started making fun of my body. He said I'd never leave him; what could a fat lard like me ever do on my own? He said all the cellulite on my butt made it look like scrambled eggs. I said, 'Well, you better kiss my sunny side now because it's the last time you'll see it!' I already had a bag packed and in my car. I borrowed some money from my parents to help me move, and the rest is history."

"Emma ..."

"So, that's where the name came from. My final revenge. I moved up here to New York to start over. That's where everyone starts over, right? I opened Sunny Side several years ago and I've been my own woman ever since. He's the rooster, you know? I drew a caricature of his ugly mug, just so the world could see how hideous he was. I always thought he looked like a cross between a toad and a pelican, so I slapped a rooster comb on him and called it a day."

She was even more beautiful than she'd been an hour ago, now that he knew her scars. How had it happened that they'd gotten so comfortable with each other so fast?

"Oh gosh, listen to me, word vomiting all over you. I'm sorry, I don't usually do that to strangers."

"Don't ever apologize to me, Emma. I'm so sorry for everything that's happened to you. For what it's worth, I think ..." *What am I going to say, exactly?* "I think you're incredibly beautiful and inspiring."

Emma turned and looked into his eyes. They were a light brown, with flecks of green and gold in them. Almost hazel, but Peter saw in her gaze a world of emotions. She wasn't broken, she wasn't even a little bit self-conscious. She was a fierce and determined fighter, and gone were the days when she was going to accept less than she deserved from anyone. He felt something stir in him, something he hadn't felt in a long time.

Her face softened towards him, but she avoided acknowledging his compliment. "I think that's why I cook. When I think about him, I get mad and just want to punch something. So, I punch dough. Or I create a cake. You can't get mad at a cake. You have to nurture it, encourage it, and take the time with it. You can't just throw it on a board and expect it to come together."

"I guess that's true."

"What about you, what's your story?"

"I lost the love of my life several years ago."

"I'm sorry, Peter. May I ask how it happened?"

"She married my brother. They're pregnant with their third child." Peter proceeded to tell her the whole story, including about the seagull and the wedding.

"Ouch, that hurts. That's not at all what I was expecting you to say." Her tone didn't soften. "I hate to say it, but if she married your brother, then she obviously wasn't the love of your life."

"Thanks. Do you have a sympathetic bone in your body?"

"I do, but that wouldn't do you any favors now. It is what it is. People are going to do what people are going to do, and sometimes there's no reason behind it. Most of the time, it has nothing to do with the person who gets hurt, they're just a casualty of war. It has to do with the person doing the hurting, intentional or not. You got hurt because you couldn't see what Cecelia and Mattias saw in each other. Like you were two pieces of the same puzzle, but you were both corner pieces, whereas Mattias fit right beside her. You thought you were part of the equation, but you were really just the paper they were writing on, as sad as that is to accept."

"You sort of sound like her in a way."

"Well then, I like her already. Nothing ever just happens."

"Please, save the lectures. I was having a good morning." *Crap, I've already spent the whole morning with her? Refocus, Peter. What were you talking about?* "Personality wise, you're the exact opposite of Cecelia."

"Yet we both ended up in your life. Funny, huh? The veil between worlds has lifted and the alter egos collide. I don't give lectures, I state facts …"

"I was trying to help her. I just thought she needed space. I was trying to be the bigger person."

"Well, maybe space was the problem in the first place. If I had a man who looked like you, I'd never let him out of my sight. If she was totally fine with not seeing you for days or weeks on end, then you never really had her. I think Cecelia sounds about as hard-headed as a dried-up, dead turtle."

Peter winced. Emma was brutal, but she was slicing the truth from his soul, word for word until he was bare.

"What are you doing about it now? How are you moving on?"

"I almost got fired. They sent me to therapy. So, I guess I'm in therapy. Actually, I'm not, because it's over. Now, I'm trying to live day to day, saying 'yes' to everything. Those were the instructions the therapist gave me. 'Don't be so uptight. Say "yes" to everything that comes along. Quit trying to control the situation.'" He didn't bother to tell her the part about asking women out.

"I like her, she's right. I don't know anything about a seagull, but in my experience, God is who or what you need him to be at that point. He helps those who help themselves." She paused, slowly turning her head to him. "Wait … so, you have to say 'yes' to *everything?*" *Uh oh.* The wicked glint in her eyes made Peter hot under the collar. He wasn't sure if he should stay and answer, or run away.

"Yes, because I'm—"

"Because you're too uptight. Got it. That's your schtick, right? You're Darcy. All handsomely infuriating so that I'm not supposed to know whether I want to slap your face or shove you against this tree and have my way with you. *Right?*"

Peter's mouth fell open in shock, his face turning bright red. He choked on air as his mouth went dry and something in his atmosphere massively shifted. "My … what? You want … what?"

Emma grinned knowingly at him. "I asked God for the perfect man. A reward for all my previous trouble, if you will. One day not too long ago, he walked into my bakery. He spent the better part of this morning taking care of me, and now here we are, baring our souls to each other."

Peter was touched. No woman had been this honest about how she felt about him in a long time and he wasn't exactly sure what to do about it. "I'm far from perfect."

"Not from where I'm sitting." She shifted to face him.

"Are you always this forward?"

"I am. I told you, I don't deal well with games anymore."

In a flash, Emma was in Peter's lap, pinning him to the tree. She fit against him seamlessly. With her sudden movement, Emma's hair fell down into waves around her face. His hands were at his sides as she lightly placed hers on top of them and leaned in. Peter was at a loss for words as he stared at her. Emma slowly leaned in to kiss him, lightly brushing her lips against his to let him know how much she wanted him. She smelled like sugar and flour, and she tasted like all the things he'd been missing—coffee, passion, solidarity, excitement. All Peter could think was maybe it was time he let go of Cecelia, because he was more than interested in the woman in his lap who oozed warmth and fervor for him. He wrapped his arms around Emma's waist and pulled her deeper into the kiss that she'd started.

Chapter Seven

They spent the rest of that day together, and every free minute after that. The kiss had knocked down invisible barriers, releasing a flood of openness and connection unrivalled with any other human being he'd ever met. Peter reveled in Emma's brashness, and willingness to state what she wanted and what she expected from life and from those around her. She told him exactly how she felt, and exactly how he made her feel, which in turn paved the way to show him how she expected him to talk about his feelings. Her forwardness was an enigma to him at first, but as he got used to it, he started to crave her truth.

When she wasn't fired up about something, she was soft and warm. They spent most evenings cuddled up on the couch in each other's arms, falling asleep to *Jeopardy!* reruns. She cooked dinner or brought him leftovers every night, and every morning he'd wake up early enough to cook her breakfast before she had to be at work. Emma started going to work slightly later, so that she and Peter could walk to work together every morning. She also coordinated her off days to match his, so they could soak up every second together. Four months in, Peter called Mattias.

"Hej! I haven't heard from you for a while. How've you been? *Where've* you been? Under a rock?"

"I met someone."

A noticeable silence for a few seconds answered him at first, and then, "That's really great, Peter. What's her name?" Peter gave him a quick rundown of their relationship.

"Why don't you bring her over to dinner this Friday? Cecelia and I would love to meet her."

*****

Emma was more nervous than Peter thought she'd be. Emma was aware of what a monumental moment this was in any relationship, especially one with the previously reserved Peter Levander, and she was nervous of meeting 'the other woman' in his life. Not his mother – she wasn't nervous to meet Astrid at all – but the one who'd previously captured his heart. Mattias greeted them at the gallery door. Long gone was the Life and Death gallery in Cecelia's studio. Now it was replaced with a City Lights theme.

"Oh wow, she really is talented!" Emma had never been much into photography, but she could clearly see that these photos weren't just quick, ill-thought-out snapshots.

"Emma's an artist, too," Peter beamed. "She makes edible sculptures you. Would. Not. Believe." He emphasized the words as he proudly placed his arm around her waist. "She's really gifted. And she makes the most fabulous breakfast foods you've ever put in your mouth." He kissed the top of her head.

Mattias grinned at his brother. He never thought he'd see the day when Peter had turned into a pile of mush. "I have no doubt."

Cecelia waddled to the door when she heard their voices on the stairs. She was about to pop any day now; her due date was only three weeks away. Charlie and Ellie were playing loudly in their playpen and stopped to look up. Charlie stood up, immediately raising his hands over his head to be picked up. Ellie tried to copy her brother and fell back into the playpen in a fit of laughter. Peter walked over and picked Charlie up, kissing his chubby face in the process. He put him down and Charlie zoomed off, running straight into Mattias' leg. "He's just a ball of energy. I think he's going to be an athlete."

Emma laughed as she watched Peter, who was now holding Ellie. Ellie had her little arms thrown around his neck, clinging to him for dear life and laughing all the while. "He's the love of her life. We don't even matter to her," Cecelia mused, as Emma felt a twinge in her heart.

"Unc!" Ellie squealed.

"Look at you! You've almost got a full word out!" Peter glowed at her, looking around the room.

"Yep and she says 'Da', too!" Mattias added. "Not much else is legible, yet. But she's usually very serious about it, nonetheless. I think she's going to be a lawyer."

"Quit it," Cecelia poked Mattias in his ribs. "I want them to find their own paths, not the paths we choose for them."

"Yes, dear. I'm starving!"

Cecelia turned to Emma and said, "Peter tells us you're a fantastic cook. We're so happy to have you, but please don't judge us too harshly. Sometimes it's all I can do to get a bowl of Cheerios happening. Mattias is the real cook here, I mostly just stir stuff."

"I'm sure whatever you made will be perfect," Emma replied politely.

Mattias and Peter set the kids up in their high chairs with raviolis and non-spill juice cups, while Emma helped Cecelia carry the food to the table. There was salad, garlic bread, and some sort of large casserole that smelled amazing.

"It's been a long time since I had a casserole like this. It reminds me of something my grandma would make back home in Alabama," Emma said.

"Oh! You're from Alabama? I'm from Georgia!" Cecelia squealed with delight. Endless chatter commenced and it was settled. They were instantly bonded. Mattias and Peter made eye contact with each other from across the table, grinned, and raised their glasses in a silent toast.

Chapter Eight

The next few weeks, Emma was markedly more emotional. Peter asked if she wanted to talk about anything, but she always said she didn't really know what was wrong, she was just sad. The dinner with Mattias and Cecelia prompted more frequent talks about the future, as if there were an unspoken agreement between them that they'd already decided on.

"You realize I can't have kids, right?"

"You realize I'm too old to have kids, right?"

He was trying to make her feel better. Emma laughed a deep, throaty laugh, overemphasizing to hide her broken heart. Since meeting his niece and nephew, she also seemed to be a little insecure. "Men are never 'too old' to have kids. Biology is cruel like that. We get like a hundred eggs or something to use before we're thirty, and you get a trillion sperms to use before you're ninety-nine. How is that fair?" Peter kissed her neck. She'd mentioned several times how much she'd wanted to be a mom, and how much she missed her baby.

The next week, Peter came home to a locked bathroom.

"Emma?" Sobs. "Emma, are you all right?" More sobs. Peter rammed into the door, busting it down. Emma was lying crumpled on the bathroom tiles, crying into a towel. Peter looked around. Nothing was evidently wrong, except she was holding a wadded-up piece of paper in her hand, moist with her tears.

"Emma? Emma, what's wrong?" Peter crawled onto the floor, scooping her up in his arms as she cried into his chest. She shoved the piece of paper into his hand, said something he couldn't make out, and started sobbing profusely into him again as he held her tighter.

After what seemed like hours, because Peter's legs had fallen asleep from sitting on the cold, hard tiles, Emma had finally calmed down enough to where he could halfway understand what she was saying.

"You, you, you know how I went to, to, to the doctor's this, this morning?" she stuttered out, as she tried to catch her breath. Massive crystalline tears rolled down her cheeks as she looked up into Peter's ice-blue eyes. The paper she'd given him was completely unsalvageable and had long since fallen from his hand, disintegrating into soggy confetti on the floor.

"I'm sorry I wasn't able to go with you. I'll be better for you." He'd asked, but had been unable to get out of work, having just gotten back into Petrov's good graces. Emma hid her head in his shoulder, sobbing loudly again and continuing to do so for the next thirty minutes. Peter stood up, and picked Emma up with him, carrying her to the bed. He would at least make her more comfortable if she couldn't find her words yet.

The next morning, Peter woke up to an empty bed. He sat up, realizing he was still in his work clothes from the day before. He pulled his jacket and button-up shirt off, leaving just his dress pants and his undershirt. Noticing Emma wasn't in the bathroom either, he went to find her.

Emma was sitting quietly at the table, with a bowl of plain oatmeal in front of her. Gruel. It was untouched, and likely cold. There was a lump of butter beside the bowl, sliced but never placed on its destination. Emma was quietly staring at a coffee mug, lost in her thoughts. Peter sat down beside her and placed his hands over hers.

"Do you want to talk about it?"

"I just thought there'd be more time."

"More time?"

"The doctor … the doctor said the reason I've been so emotional is because I have … P.O.I." She had remained calm until she spoke the last initial. Tears were again streaming profusely down her face, mirroring last night. Peter wrapped his arms around her shoulders, pulling her into him. Emma gripped him for dear life as she continued to sob. Finally, she caught a breath, long enough to explain to him.

"Premature ovarian insufficiency. Early menopause. I knew that realistically I could never have kids after what happened, but I still hoped, you know? I had this stupid idea that all I needed was time, and the right man in my life. I got all hopeful around Charlie and Ellie, and seeing you with them. But my body re, re, rejected me anyway." She collapsed back into him as he held her tighter.

Peter felt his heart twist into knots for her. This woman, this goddess in his arms, had been planning to have his children. They hadn't said 'I love you' to each other yet, but in a way they didn't have to. It was unspoken between them, and she had just confirmed any miniscule doubts he'd still had.

"Sshhhh, it's ok. Your family is the people you choose it to be, biological or otherwise. We're going to adopt so many kids, we'll have to move into a schoolhouse." Emma slowly looked up at him, her face splotchy and her eyes swollen and red. "I love you, Emma," Peter said, as he kissed her damp face.

Chapter Nine

"I really need your help. Can you just come with me? I have no idea what I'm doing and I'm honestly terrified."

"I mean, are you sure you wouldn't rather Cecelia help you?" Mattias asked. "She'd be so much better at this than I would and she'd appreciate the fresh air." Cecelia had given birth to their third child, Elizabeth Grace, the previous week. She was still very sore, but she was always energetic and had rebounded quickly after the previous two pregnancies.

"No, I think it'd be awkward and I really think she'd start crying. I can't handle two emotional women. Oh, and don't tell Cecelia, either. I don't want her accidentally letting it slip when they're having one of their chats."

"Tell me about it. Ok, I'll meet you in an hour. One thing I know for sure, you'd better decide your limit unless you're prepared to spend an entire mortgage just on the ring itself."

Peter googled jewelry stores, and made a short list of the ones with the highest customer ratings. He was certain he didn't want to get Emma an emerald like Cecelia had. They were opposite women, if not exactly the same. Even though it'd only been a few weeks, Emma and Cecelia had already had a lunch date and several phone calls. Peter was grateful for that. He knew how lonely each of them had been without a girlfriend in the city, what with Shelly so far away in Savannah and Emma's sisters in Alabama. Cecelia had quickly accepted her as her sister before Peter had even realized that was the next step.

The first store on the list was one Peter had seen on television and numerous billboards around the city. It wasn't Tiffany's but he reckoned it was almost as fancy as you could get. The doorman was wearing a tux, and offered Peter and Mattias tiny bottles of sparkling water. Glass bottles, no less. A saleswoman came over to assist them promptly, and then the two men were sucked into the glitz and glitter of delight.

"What does she do for a living?" the saleslady asked Peter, pulling out a small stationery pad to take notes if need be.

"She's a chef. Well, she's an entrepreneur. Actually, she's an artist," Peter answered, stumbling over his words.

"She's quite a lot of things. She owns and operates a restaurant," Mattias jumped in, trying to save his drowning brother.

"Ah, I see. An independent woman. What are her other characteristics? Tastes?"

Peter looked at the saleswoman, like a deer in headlights. "Uuuhhh …" She looked to Mattias for clarification, who was clearly enjoying watching his brother flounder.

"She's classic, but not too classic. She's very colorful, in her clothing and in her language. She's straightforward, and goes after what she wants." He turned knowingly to Peter, who was blushing. Peter hadn't told him about the tree, but had Emma told Cecelia? Most likely. He'd walked in not so long ago to hear her giggling like a schoolgirl, and she'd gotten suspiciously quiet when she noticed him watching her.

"Well, we just got a new shipment in, never before seen. It's pretty unique, let me go get it for you."

"I'll bet she says that to all the customers," Mattias said flatly, unamused.

Just a few short minutes later, the saleswoman returned holding a small gray rectangle, with a variety of colors wedged in between gray padded rows. "These are new arrivals from the Exclusive Collection. All original stones, not lab-created. Also optional, since this is an engagement ring, we could replace the stone with a diamond. You'll keep the stone, of course, as you'll have paid for it. You could stick it in a necklace or something. But we could replace it with a diamond of your choosing if you'd like to make it more official-feeling. Not every woman will say 'yes' to an aquamarine engagement ring." Her nose wrinkled, as if she'd offended herself at the mere utterance of those words.

She was right. Peter thought most of them looked gaudy and ugly, more like costume jewelry than anything. Until he noticed the one hiding silently in the corner of the rainbow, as if trying to distance itself from its more flamboyant counterparts. It had a silver band, whereas the rest were gold or rose gold. It had scrollwork inlaid into the band, delicate and subtle. The stone in it was a large milky ruby, which made Peter think of someone pouring milk into cranberry juice. It had a smaller pearl on either side of it. "That's it. That's the one," Peter said, taking it out and holding it up. "But you're right, it needs to be a diamond." The saleswoman's eyes gleamed with thoughts of commission as she excused herself for another moment, returning with a large padded envelope filled with smaller padded envelopes marked with colors.

"Now, in the diamond world there are colors. I'd suggest you don't go with a white diamond to accent this ring. You absolutely can, of course, but based on your description of her, you shouldn't. This ring is a thing of beauty, and should be complimented with an equally stunning counterpart to knock her off her feet." She proceeded to line up several options to start out with. Peter felt himself seize up again, seeing the tiny Ziploc bags arranged before him.

"Let's start with what she doesn't like, shall we?" the saleswoman suggested, encouraging him to speak. He glanced over at Mattias, who was clearly loving the fact that this little woman had completely disarmed his older brother with a bunch of tiny rocks. "Not pink. Not blue."

Two rows of bags were zipped away, like a deck of cards on a casino table. "Not orange. That's gaudy. She doesn't like gaudy. She'd like elegant, something that would go with everything but also be significantly different," Peter assured, finding his footing.

"Ah, the gentleman speaks." Several more colors were quickly filed into the bag, leaving white, yellow, brown, and gray. "White is the traditional option, but also the most commonly bought. Brown is the trendiest option, but the most commonly found in nature, though that doesn't detract from its beauty. I believe you mentioned food is her industry, so a nice chocolate diamond might befit her. Yellow is our next option.”

“That would look like a poached egg on her finger,” Mattias whispered into Peter’s ear.

The saleswoman snickered. “Moving on then. That brings us to our last color, the gray. The gray is the strong and silent of the diamond family. Not as popular, yet often more stunning. It can change colors in the light, and as with all diamonds, they do come in a variety of color ranges. The light gray resembles a white diamond, so much so that the naked eye can barely notice the difference.” She reached into the padded envelope marked ‘gray.’ “However, you can get them noticeably darker as well. This one is classified as ‘fancy gray.’ It’s not the darkest, but it’s the darkest I have available to show you. We can order anything else you might like to see.”

She held it under the light, in clamped tweezers so that Peter could see it against the ring. Beside the pearls, the reflections each gave the other were shades of white and dark, changing with every glance. Shadows and light playing out in one tiny ring, past and present colliding to create a beautiful future. “No, that won’t be necessary. This is absolutely the one.”

Peter didn't even look at the price tag, which might've been a mistake but he didn't really care. He was only doing this once. Well, technically twice, but this time it was going to be right. As Peter handed the saleswoman his credit card, he thought he heard her give a little squeal of delight. No doubt he was paying several months' rent for her, at least.

"This has been entertaining to say the least, but I've got to get back to Cecelia. Charlie started one of his terrible twos tantrums right before I left," Mattias said, hugging Peter. "I'm really proud of you."

"Thank you, and thanks for coming with me. We'll see you on Friday for dinner? I think Emma's making a trifle or something she saw in a magazine." Friday dinners were a new tradition Emma and Cecelia had decided to instate this week.

"Sure thing. I'll let C know. See ya then!" Mattias waved and walked out of the jewelry store.

The saleswoman returned. "All right, Mr. Levander, we're all set. We'll have that gorgeous new stone in its setting for you in about a week's time. I'll give you a call when it's ready. And after she says 'yes,' bring her in and we'll resize it if need be. That and the warranty is all included. Don't lose the receipt." She barked the last sentence, as if it were a common occurrence in the lucrative world of jewelry warranties.

Peter walked out of the jewelry store on Cloud Nine. Letting his mind wander, he thought that if he ever opened a jewelry store chain, it would be called Cloud Nine. *I wonder if anybody's ever thought of that? I'm sure they have. What were some of the names in that post I saw that one time? Thai Tanic? Bread Pitt? I think my favorite was the chiropractic office called Thorassic Park. No, actually my favorite is Sunny Sides. I love that woman. She'll say yes. Won't she? I think she will. Why wouldn't she? What if she doesn't? She will. How am I going to propose? It's got to be something really awesome. Maybe I'll cook for her. No, that's too risky. I could burn it, that's happened more than plenty of times. OH! I've got it. Brilliant, Peter, just brilliant. She won't even see it coming. She'll …*

A smile wider than three lanes of traffic was across Peter's face as he stepped out onto the crosswalk, not noticing the crowd of people who had not gone with him. He barely heard the horn as the bus plowed into him.

Chapter Ten

There was nothing but darkness. Then pain. Muffled sounds from unfamiliar voices. Shooting pains through his leg and back. Something on his face. Bright lights, medical speak, then more darkness. Sore muscles, headaches, and more pain that faded in and out with his consciousness. Occasionally, there was a faint beep from somewhere in the distance. He felt a touch on his hand as light as a feather and a million miles away. A man's voice, somewhere in the distance. Crying, sobbing. A toddler was mumbling somewhere a football stadium's length away. His body ached all over, though he couldn't feel any of his limbs. He was cold, and tired of being in the dark. He tried to open his eyes, but nothing happened. Another voice, a woman's, said, "Eyes fluttering." He loved that voice. He couldn't think what her name was, but he instinctively knew he belonged to her. Then the voice was gone for what felt like years.

The man's voice was back, along with another man's voice. Peter couldn't hear what they were saying; they sounded like they were underwater. He wanted to scream at them to talk normal, but no sound came out. Later, the woman's voice was back, whispering so quietly that he could barely hear her in the blackness of his surroundings before he went to sleep again.

When he woke up, the feather feeling was touching his hand. He tried to look at his hands but he couldn't see his body at all. He went back to sleep.

*****

The next time Peter woke up, he was back at the lake in the Poconos. He couldn't remember how he had got here, or when. He could smell the chargrilled smell of the steaks on the grill, and he felt his stomach growl. He sat down at the picnic table to wait for them.

Peter's whole body throbbed, but he couldn't remember doing any sort of physical activity that would've warranted such a reaction. Temporarily, he thought maybe he'd just slept wrong. He heard a woman's voice coming from somewhere, but he couldn't remember coming up here with anyone. In fact, he was sure he hadn't come up here with anyone. Had he just had some long dream of Emma? Had he not even met her yet? His heart broke a little bit for the woman in the restaurant. No, that wasn't right, either. They clearly knew each other; his memories of her were as real and as clear as ... as ...

Peter looked around. As clear as what was in front of him? The landscape was an impressionist's expression of nature. The lake was wavy, swirling navy and emerald. There was no sunlight, only a colorful collage of blues and whites, swirled together like a Van Gogh painting. The trees swayed upwards in a similar fashion, but they were shades of fall instead of the spring shades Peter had seen when he was here before. *That's odd.*

Peter heard a commotion beside him, and looked over to see the same seagull had returned again. "I already said I'm not feeding you."

"I'm not here for food, you ninny. I'm here for you," the seagull said, staring him down.

"What the—since when can you talk?" Peter stuttered out.

"I've always been able to talk in whatever form I choose. We've met before, you know. A lot."

Peter got up and started pacing back and forth on the patio, running his hands through his hair in the process.

"What's happening to me?"

"We needed to have a chat."

Peter started laughing hysterically. "Yeah, I get it, God is a seagull. Don't you have better things to do, like finding crumbs in a parking lot?"

"Not right now. I penciled you in. Listen, I'm sorry I threw you under the bus. Literally!" The seagull's head rolled back, eyes squinted and its beak opened, falling up and down, as the bird's wing reached under to cradle its stomach. With each tremor of its beak, a small squeak escaped.

"I didn't know seagulls could laugh, much less crack themselves up. Do you know how ridiculous you look?" Peter muttered.

"Fine, fine." And in a flash, the seagull was replaced by a young man. He had wavy brown hair, a light stubble, and eyes that crinkled in the corners. His cerulean blue eyes sparkled like they could peer into anyone's soul and see their authentic self. He looked vaguely familiar, but Peter couldn't place him.

"I know you from somewhere. Are we dead?"

"DUDE! We don't use the 'D' word around here! It's a real downer," the man shushed Peter. "You're peachy keen, and I'm 'Ethereally Elevated,'" he said in air quotes. "We have T-shirts and everything. God sent me as a messenger. He said it might be easier on you, since you don't deal so well with the bird."

"So, I got hit by a bus, but I'm not gone?" The more Peter was in this alternate reality, the more he was starting to remember his actual reality. Emma had not been a dream, or rather she'd been the best dream he never wanted to wake up from. He remembered holding her on the bathroom tiles, shopping for the ring, and then there was a brief vision of the bus before everything went pitch black.

"Nah, man. You've got too much else to do. You broke your leg when you bounced off the bus …" Peter cringed but the man kept going. "And you tore your spleen, so those had to be fixed. You got a minor concussion, what with the whole getting hit by a bus and bouncing on the pavement thing. The bus driver saw you almost in time. He was about to turn the corner when you stepped out in front of him, so he was going super slow but, you know, it's still a bus. You're super lucky it was nothing major, overall. You're gonna be all right. It'll just suck for a few weeks till you recoup. You're all looped out from the anesthesia right now …" He did a makeshift tap dance, with his arms coming out to the side. "Enter us."

"Great, so nothing serious," Peter quipped. "What's the message?"

"Look, He knows you believe and try to do right, but He also knows that deep down you're pissed off and stubborn to the core. Cecelia looks for signs. You require a more direct approach to the world. How often did you see the seagull at her apartment? All the time, right? But every time, you just saw a bird, whereas she saw a whole revelation. So, you got a bus."

"Gee, thanks."

The man shrugged, holding his hands palm up and level with his shoulders in an overly dramatic gesture. "It is what it is. You're fine; it's just gonna hurt really bad to walk for a few weeks. But you got the message. Oh, no you didn't. Ok, the message. Here's what's going to happen, the Grand Design, if you will. Are you ready?"

"As ready as I'll ever be, I suppose. Is this my *It's a Wonderful Life* moment?"

"Something like that. Here goes. You were always supposed to fall in love with Cecelia, so that she could fall in love with Mattias. Everything that's happened, it was always supposed to happen that way. Especially the hard parts. Emma was always made for you. Walk with me," the man said, as he opened the cabin door for Peter. They stepped through, but instead of the cabin's studio set-up, they were in a hospital room. A faint beeping was in the background, as Peter watched Emma massaging a lifeless version of himself on a hospital bed.

"Look at her, massaging your arms so that your muscles don't atrophy," the man said, as Peter watched her. Streaks of teardrops had dried on either side of her face, leaving trails through her foundation in their wake. She gently closed Peter's inert fingers around a one-pound weight, lifting and stretching his arm. She did this about thirty times, before she moved to the other hand. When she was done, she moved to the unbroken leg, and lifted it up ever so gently so as not to jiggle his injuries or incisions.

"How long have I been here?" Peter asked, concerned.

"Three days. It feels like longer because of the anesthesia and the concussion. You're not going to atrophy because you're going home tomorrow, but she doesn't know that. Only you and I do. She's been so stressed out that she's doing anything she can think of to help you. That's true love, someone who watches out for your best interests even when you can't see it. She'll move your good leg for exactly a mile. She and Mattias take shifts; he sits with you all day and she sits with you all night. The rational part of them knows you shouldn't be in here for too long, but that doesn't make it any easier. Mattias hasn't told her about the ring, though he wants to. He's afraid if he does, then you'll wake up and be mad, but if he doesn't then you won't wake up and she'll be shattered that she didn't know. She'll blame herself, thinking if she'd told you 'yes,' you would've recovered and come back to her."

Peter was in tears now, watching her. "But we won't go down that rabbit hole, because that's not how your story is going to play out, is it?" The man slapped Peter on his back and he winced, feeling the pain from the earthly surgery he'd had.

"So, here's how it's gonna play out, my man. You'll be fine, and you'll come out on top. Better than ever, because you're gonna listen to everything I'm saying and not fight me on it, right?"

"Ok."

"Ok. You're going to marry Emma asap. That schoolhouse full of kids you told her the two of you would adopt? You're going to do that, too. And get a good lawyer soon, who really knows business. Money won't be an issue, because not only will she open two other restaurants in the city, but within five years it'll be franchised in a hundred locations across the country. Your wife will be the queen of breakfast food. You can stay at your job for a while, but eventually you'll have to quit. You'll be happy to quit, because you're going to have to help her raise the ten kids. You're great with kids, so you won't mind.

"You'll die in your bed an old man, with twenty grandkids around you and your wife in your arms. Not long after, she'll join you. Oh, and have Mattias design a better logo than that ugly rooster."

"Wow … how do I know you're telling the truth?"

"You really are dense, sometimes. Tell Cecelia my corneas went to a blind guy who now trains seeing eye dogs. You don't usually get to hear the rest of the story. It's really kind of a beautiful system once you get to see the other side," the man said, pausing for a moment, as if reminiscing on his previous life. "Oh, and here's something else. Tell Cecelia that it was always me sitting beside her in the graveyard when she was taking photos, trying to find me. If she looks closely, I'm in every one." Peter's mouth fell open in realization.

"Or maybe don't tell her, it's up to you. We both know how easily she can cry."

"You're Charlie." Peter could understand why her late husband had been so hard for Cecelia to get over. He was easy to talk to and feel comfortable around. His carefree charm and laid-back personality reminded Peter a lot of Mattias, in a way.

"Sure am."

"Why'd you tell me how I'd be 'Ethereally Elevated' later on?" Peter asked with air quotes, mimicking Charlie's from earlier.

"Because nobody told me. If I'd known, I would've loved Cecelia ten times harder. I would've spent more time with her and gone on twenty dates a week just to hear her laugh. I really do want to thank you for taking care of her after, you know. You did everything exactly right, you need to know that and forgive yourself of any lingering doubts. You're a pretty good guy. Not as hot as me, obviously, but you're all right." He punched Peter lightly on the arm before turning to leave.

"Hey, Charlie?"

"Yeah?"

"Will I see you again? Or God?"

"Nah, man. Not till the end."

*****

In a flash, Peter's eyes fluttered open. His vision was blurry, and he was in a lot of pain. Emma's head was lying on the bed, her arms entwined around his arm for dear life. Her hair was fanned out over his shoulder, and he could hear the faintest of snores coming from the side of her head that he couldn't see.

"Mmmmma," Peter tried to speak but it came out more like a hum. He tried again, searching for the energy to put into his voice this time. "EmmmmMA."

Her head moved, but she didn't wake up. Peter was starting to get tired again, so he put his last effort into the arm she was clinging to. His hand twitched, just enough to make her wake from her slumber. Peter's eyes rolled in his head but he tried desperately to hold onto his reality.

"Peter? Peter! Nurse! Nurse!" Emma ran to the door to get a nurse to check his vitals before returning to his side. "How're you feeling?"

Peter was tired, but he was trying desperately to hang onto his thought process before the drugs took him under again. "Wweeee need to get married today."

Chapter Eleven

Emma called Mattias immediately to tell him Peter was awake, and to tell him what Peter's first words had been. She heard him relay the message to Cecelia in the background, followed by a squeal. "I know a guy!" Cecelia screamed loud enough for Emma to hear on the other end of the line.

Two hours later, Mattias, Cecelia, and someone Emma was quite familiar with showed up. Each was carrying a child.

"Roger! What're you doing here?" Emma ran up and hugged him and little Charlie, who reached out for her when he saw her.

"I married these two, an' Cecelia thought I could marry ye as well!" Roger said cheerfully in his Irish accent.

"Wait, how do you two know each other?" Cecelia asked.

"I wrote about her on me food blog! She makes the best pancakes I've ever had!"

*****

"Maybe I shouldn't tell you this, but I feel like you should know. He had just bought a ring right before it happened. It's still at the shop waiting on him, but I don't know what prompted him to skip a step," Mattias whispered to Emma as they waited in the chapel. "He usually never does anything unscripted."

It was the most informal of ceremonies. Peter was fully awake as the nurses got him up and into a wheelchair, and rolled him down to the in-house chapel. Emma was still in her uniform, which she'd basically worked and slept in since Peter had been in the hospital. Peter was in his hospital gown, and Emma pulled a chair up beside his wheelchair so they could be equals. A stained-glass cross behind the altar was their only decoration as Roger took his place in front of the small crowd. Cecelia sat on the pew on Emma's side with Elizabeth Grace, and Mattias sat on Peter's side with Charlie and Ellie.

Quiet vows filled a quiet ceremony, other than the random baby noises made by Elizabeth. When they got home the next day, a fancy bag was waiting on the kitchen counter.

"I had Mattias go by and pick it up; I didn't want to wait any longer to give it to you. There's something that goes with it, though." He hobbled on his crutches over to the bookshelf where he kept his drawings. "I was planning on doing this big elaborate picnic under our tree and giving you this, but Chinese takeout will have to do." He inched back to her, holding a single drawing. "I did this before I knew anything about you other than your name. I just kept going back, because it felt like home." He handed her the drawing and then slowly moved towards the refrigerator to pull out the fresh bag of Chinese food he'd had Mattias pick up on the way.

Emma gasped. "Peter … this is amazing. This is perfect, really." It was the painstakingly detailed, colored-pencil drawing of the inside of Sunny Sides that he'd done while he was in therapy.

*****

Emma attended every session of physical therapy with Peter until he had made a full recovery. After that, they invited Peter and Mattias' parents and their brother Caspar, along with Emma's two sisters and parents, to a late wedding reception at Mattias and Cecelia's studios. Peter thought about that kiss against the tree all the time … If he was honest with himself, completely honest, that was the moment he knew he was going to marry Emma.

Emma had come into his life exactly when he'd needed her the most, and saved him from the darkest depths of himself. He could hardly harbor resentment against Cecelia and Mattias anymore, because he finally understood what their love had meant to them. If Cecelia wasn't his sister-in-law, he seriously doubted he'd even still think of her. He loved her, but only in the way of a friend and brother now. Emma had captured his heart completely, and she hadn't been shy about wanting it.

Chapter Twelve

"I'm really sorry for how I acted before," Peter said to Cecelia on her balcony the night of the reception. It was almost October, and she had brought blankets out for both of them to wrap up in. Peter had said he needed a minute to talk to her, just the two of them. "I understand now, and I'm so sorry that I didn't before."

"Really, Peter, it's ok."

"No, I acted like a total jerk. I should've been more open and I apologize for putting you in that situation. I wanted to talk to you about something else, though. When I was in the hospital, I saw Charlie."

"Yes, he sat on your bed and hugged you. We brought all of them, hoping you'd hear them and feel better."

"No, not baby Charlie. Charlie, your late husband Charlie."

Cecelia backed up to the chair slowly, putting her hand on the wrought iron outdoor table. "You, you saw Charlie? Peter, did you almost d-die?" she stuttered, as tears welled up in her eyes.

"He said you'd start crying," Peter said lightheartedly, and Cecelia laughed, tears pooling on her cheeks before rolling down and bouncing onto the blanket wrapped around her.

"He also said they call it 'Ethereally Elevated.' They don't use the 'D' word up there."

"Yeah, that sounds exactly like him," Cecelia said; she was profusely crying now.

"He wanted me to tell you, there's a guy who got his eyes. He trains seeing eye dogs now. And I asked him for proof that I wasn't dreaming. He told me something only you can verify. All those times you went to the cemetery looking for him, trying to take pictures to capture his spirit? He said to tell you he was sitting by you the whole time, and that if you look carefully, you'll see he's in all of them."

By now, Cecelia was crying like Peter had never seen a woman cry. She wrapped herself tighter in her blanket right as Mattias stepped out onto the balcony.

"Crap, what'd you do to her?" Mattias asked, as he went and wrapped his arms around his soggy wife.

*****

Cecelia couldn't sleep that night. She tossed and turned, replaying Peter's words over and over in her head. Finally, she couldn't take it anymore. She switched the light on as Mattias continued to snore, his face buried almost completely in his pillow. Cecelia walked over to the closet and pulled up a ladder to reach into the corner. She felt around on her tiptoes until finally she reached the photo albums and box of photos from the time before. The time before she ever thought she could be happy again.

Slowly, she went through every picture on each page of the album, not believing her eyes. Photography was her profession, her passion. She'd seen each of these photos thousands of times before; how was it possible that she'd never put the pieces together? She moved on to the box of unkempt photos, finding the same, identical results.

When Mattias woke up the next morning, his wife was asleep on the floor, a halo of photographs strewn around her. Her face was red and swollen from finally crying herself to sleep. Mattias lightly shook her awake.

"Cecelia, what's all this?"

"Just look, Mattias. Look at them all." The only other person on Earth who would understand the gravity of the pictures would be her precious husband.

Mattias picked up a handful of photos, shuffling through them faster and faster until his eyes were as wide as hers had been the night before. Somewhere, somehow, in each and every single picture, a seagull was looking back.

The End

For now...

A Note from the Author

These characters have become like a second family to me. Originally, *The Weight of Birds* was going to be a standalone book.

However, due to overwhelming response and requests for a sequel, I reconsidered my original plan. This *Still Waters* novella was born, and you might notice somewhere on whatever platform you bought this book, it's now listed as being part of a series – The Levander Brothers: Book One and Book Two.

There's still a third brother, and there are even more stories to pursue. Thank you to everyone who's bought a copy of either, and thank you for loving my characters as much as I do.

Stay tuned!

Acknowledgements

I'd like to thank God for giving me the courage to follow my creativeness, and for picking me to be the one to tell these stories.

Thank you to my sweet husband, parents, friends, family and hometown for being so enthusiastically supportive of my creative endeavors.

Thank you to my store and my work team for being such awesome cheerleaders and supporters.
Oprah hasn't called. (Yet!)

Last but certainly not least, thank you to my editor, Mark Swift, and to my A-team: Kristen, Elizabeth, Ms. Diane, Ashley F. H., and Kayla. You guys help to make me the best writer I can possibly be and I love you dearly for it!

Cover design by Paper & Sage

Thank you for reading!
If you enjoyed it, please leave a review.

Please follow me on Facebook or Instagram for
updates on new releases!

IG @theamandalewis

www.facebook.com/theamandalewis